Before he had a chance to
quickly hide, Mr. Watt r...

The Leaf Lady

was standing over his shed...

1

"Now look here Mr. Watt, you've made **a right mess** of this place," said The Leaf Lady.

"And what's more, the old bridge has **broken**."

She pointed over her shoulder at the old bridge, as she looked around in distaste at all of Mr. Watt's unfinished inventions and discarded scrap metal.

Mr. Watt started to open his mouth
but **The Leaf Lady** interrupted ~

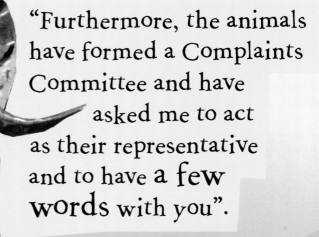

"Furthermore, the animals
have formed a Complaints
Committee and have
asked me to act
as their representative
and to have **a few
words** with you".

4

Mr. Watt filled his lungs in order to best blow **the loudest raspberry** he could muster, but he was interrupted yet again ~

5

"I don't wish to criticise your harebrained inventions", The Leaf Lady continued,

6

"I'm sure they suit YOUR purposes very well, but I'm afraid there is a limit to what WE are prepared to tolerate."

"The animals need some greener grass, so you will have to tidy up your act and repair that bridge, so they can get back across the valley."

Repairing the old bridge has been on Mr. Watt's 'to do' list for quite a while now ~ 'tidying up his act' has not.

"Harebrained? Outrageous!" he was about to splutter, when suddenly his Granddaughter Effie (Fe for short), walked round from behind the shed.

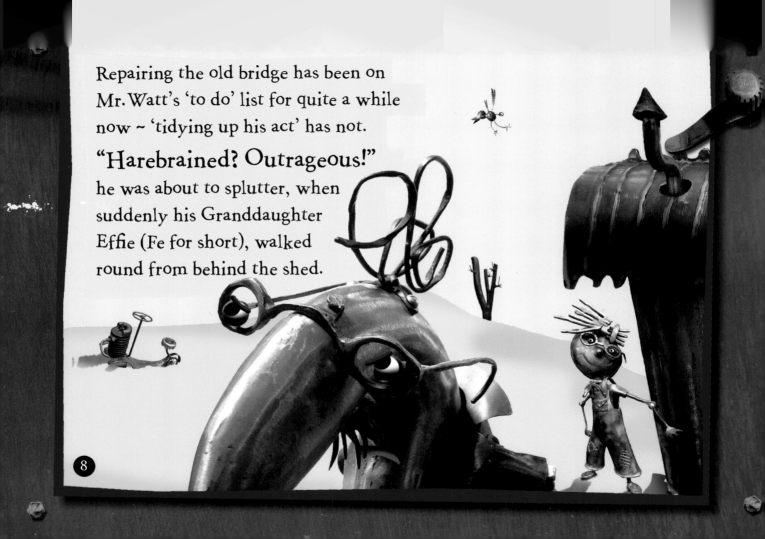

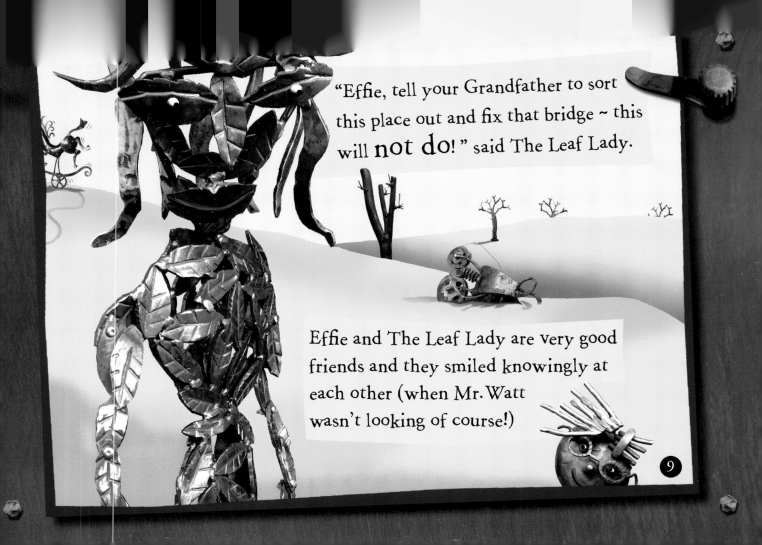

"Effie, tell your Grandfather to sort this place out and fix that bridge ~ this will **not do**!" said The Leaf Lady.

Effie and The Leaf Lady are very good friends and they smiled knowingly at each other (when Mr. Watt wasn't looking of course!)

9

Mr. Watt **looked** at Effie.
Effie **smiled** at Mr. Watt.

A sinking feeling came
over him as he realised he
wasn't going to win this one.

"Oh alright then"
he muttered.

"Come on Effie ~
bring the toolbox!"

10

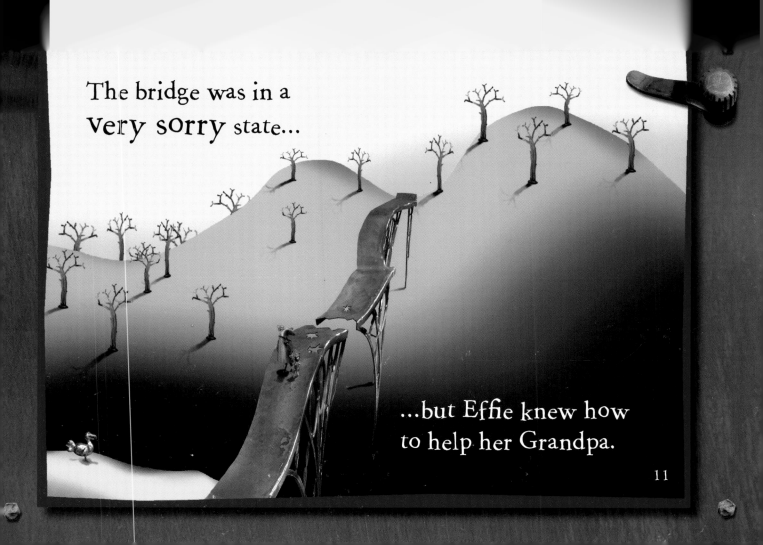

The bridge was in a **very sorry** state...

...but Effie knew how to help her Grandpa.

11

She used his spanners
for the nuts and bolts...

Effie danced and jumped for joy when the work was finished! She put up a row of bunting when all of the animals were ready to run across to the greener grass.

14

And the animals squeaked and grunted with delight as they crossed!

15

"Just make sure you look after the place from now on Mr. Watt" said The Leaf Lady ~"I'm leaving Effie in charge to keep an eye on you".

Effie smiled at The Leaf Lady...

16

But as he looked at all the animals frolicking in the greener grass, and the smile on Effie's face...

...he decided he really didn't mind anymore,
and this time he really would 'tidy up his act'!

All books available on iPad & iPhone,
and some as printed versions! Check out
and follow the links on mrwatt.biz today!

Go
Dig
Doug!

A search for
greener grass, (with
a hint of tillage...)

Posh~Dog
and his
light relief.

A wee tale of
courtesy and
satisfaction...

Mrs.
Choir
and her
concerted effort:

a tale of discord
and comeuppance!

by Jon Mills

Fe
(for short)

Mr.
Watt
and the
Abyss

Mr. Watt
& Iron Pig:

a tale of manufacturing, marketing and the environment!

Lionel,
the very cross
dresser.

by Jon Mills